Hello, I'm Big Cat.
I love to read at home.
What's your name?
Do you like reading too

Let's read together!
This book is about two
who are always arguin
I hope you enjoy it!

Follow my pawprints a
to discover lots of fun

At the end of the story
but wait and see!

If you love reading thi
come and read with me
lots more exciting things
characters to meet!

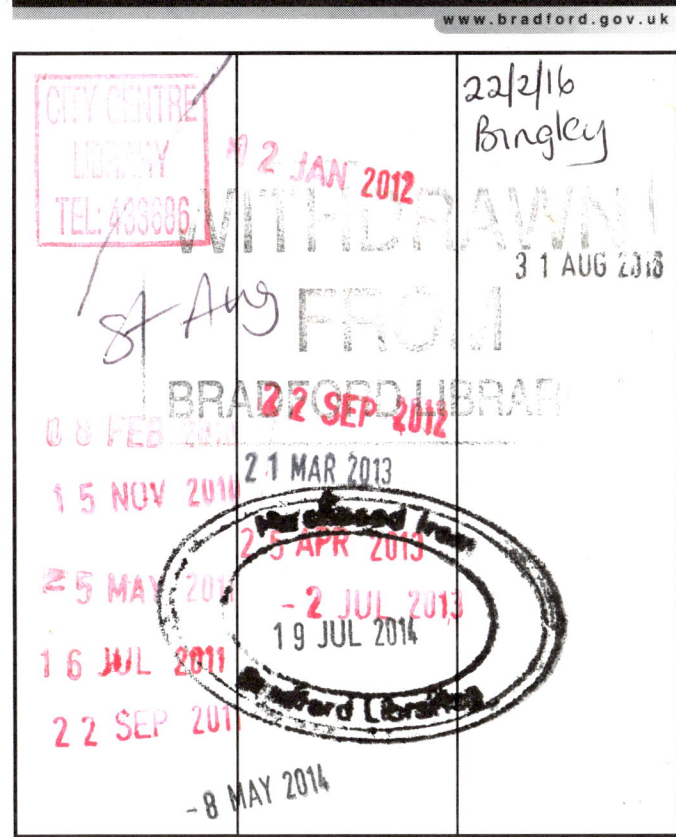

Please return/renew this item by the last date shown. Items not required other customers may be renewed phone and over the internet.

1

C Collins
Big Cat

Published by Collins
An imprint of HarperCollins*Publishers*
77–85 Fulham Palace Road
Hammersmith
London
W6 8JB

Text © 2006 Julia Donaldson
Illustration © 2006 Sholto Walker
Design © HarperCollins*Publishers* Limited 2005
This edition published in 2007

Series editor: Cliff Moon

10 9 8 7 6 5 4 3 2 1

ISBN-13 978-0-00-724453-9
ISBN-10 0-00-724453-3

British Library Cataloguing in Publication Data
A Catalogue record for this publication is available from the British Library.

Illustrator: Sholto Walker
Additional illustrator: Clare Beaton
Design manager: Nicola Kenwood @ Hakoona Matata & Anna Stasinska
Additional designer: Lodestone Publishing Limited; www.lodestonepublishing.com
Guided reading ideas author: Clare Dowdall
Educational consultant: Dr Rona Tutt

Acknowledgements
Collins would like to thank the teachers and children at the following schools who took part in the development of Collins Big Cat:

Alfred Sutton Primary School
St. Anne's Fulshaw C of E Primary School
Anthony Bek Primary School
Biddick Primary School
Britannia Primary School
Christ Church Charnock Richard C of E Primary School
Cronton C of E Primary School
Cuddington Community School
Glory Farm County Primary and Nursery School

St. John Fisher RC Primary School
Killinghall Primary School
Malvern Link C of E Primary School
Margaret Macmillan Primary School
Minet Nursery and Infant School
Norbreck Primary School
Offley Endowed Primary School
Portsdown Primary School
St. Margaret's RC Primary School
Wadebridge Community Primary School

Printed and bound by Printing Express Limited, Hong Kong

Browse the complete Collins catalogue at
www.collinseducation.com

Get the latest Collins Big Cat news at
www.collinsbigcat.com

The Pot of Gold

Written by Julia Donaldson

Illustrated by Sholto Walker

 Collins

Sandy and Bonny kept sheep.
"Too many sheep," said Bonny.
"Not enough sheep," said Sandy.
The two of them were always arguing.

4

One evening, they were busy arguing
when there was a tap at the door.

There on the doorstep stood a little man.
He wore a green hat and a ragged green coat.
His green shoes had holes in the toes.

"Can I stay here for two nights?" he asked.

"Yes," said Sandy.

"No," said Bonny.

"I can pay," said the little man. He took two gold coins out of his pocket.

"Well?" he asked. "Can I stay?"

"Yes!" said Sandy and Bonny. For once they agreed about something.

They took him to his room.

"Good night, and good luck!" said the little man.
Bonny laughed. "We never have any luck," she said.
But she was wrong.

The next day, Sandy was on the hill with the sheep when he saw a big pile of stones.

"That's funny," he said. "I can see something gleaming."

8

Sandy took away some of the stones, and he saw
a heap of gold coins!

"I'll run home and fetch a big pot to carry them in,"
he said.

He started to run down the hill. But then he stopped.

"Suppose someone finds the coins when I'm gone?"
he said to himself.

He put the stones back and stuck his stick into them,
so that he would be able to find the right place again.

10

Sandy ran home. "We're rich!" he shouted.
"Don't be so silly," said Bonny.
But then Sandy told her about the gold coins.
He grabbed a pot. "Let's go and get them!" he said.

"Don't be so silly," said Bonny again. "People will see us. Then everyone will want some of the gold."

"That's true," said Sandy. "Let's wait till it's dark."

12

Bonny put some food and water on the table.

"Just think," she said. "With all that money
we can buy a new house."

"Don't be silly," said Sandy. "We don't need
a new house. But we do need some more sheep."

"Sheep!" cried Bonny. "We've got too many sheep already. We can stop keeping sheep. And I can buy lots of new clothes."

"Clothes!" shouted Sandy. "You don't need any more clothes! You've got too many clothes already!"

He banged his fist on the table.

14

"I have not!" yelled Bonny. And she threw a chip at him.

"Missed!" shouted Sandy, and he threw a sausage at her.

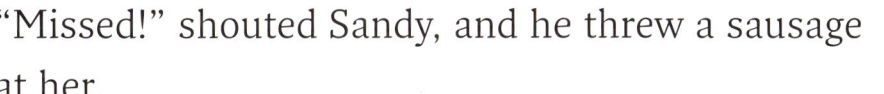

They were shouting so loudly that they didn't hear
the little man come downstairs.

"Please could you stop making so much noise?"
he asked.

16

"Oh, shut up!" yelled Bonny.

She was in such a temper that she picked up a jug of water and threw it all over the little man.

Sandy laughed.

The little man gave them both a funny look.
Then he went upstairs.

"Good night," he said. But this time he didn't say
"Good luck".

It was dark now and the moon was out.
"Let's go and get the gold," said Sandy.
They took the pot and carried it up the hill.

"There's the pile of stones with your stick in it,"
said Bonny.

She took away some of the stones. "I can't see any gold,"
she said. "You were just making it up!"

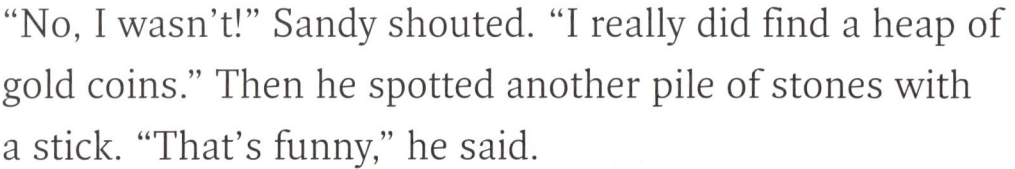

"No, I wasn't!" Sandy shouted. "I really did find a heap of gold coins." Then he spotted another pile of stones with a stick. "That's funny," he said.

Sandy and Bonny looked around them. There were hundreds of piles of stones, each one with a stick in it.

They hunted all night, but they didn't find the gold.

When they got home the little man had gone.
But there were two gold coins on the table, and a note
saying, "Keep looking".

Sandy and Bonny did keep looking. They looked every night. But they didn't find the gold.

They are still looking. And they are still arguing!

Let's talk about it!

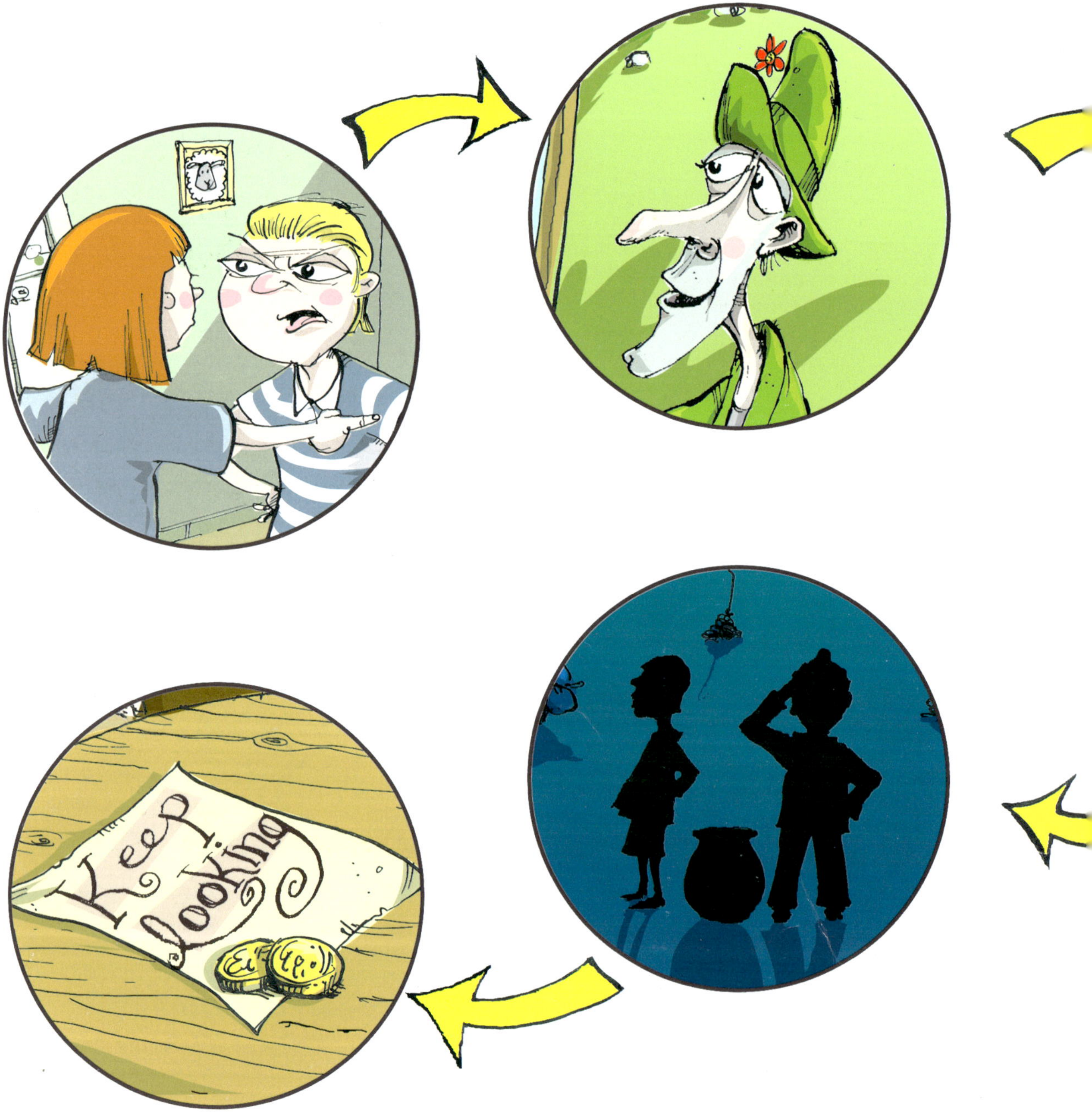

Use the pictures to retell the story. Encourage your child to follow the pictures in order and give as much detail as he or she can.

Activities

Think of a different ending for the story. On a separate piece of paper, draw pictures to show your new ending.

The Pot of Gold

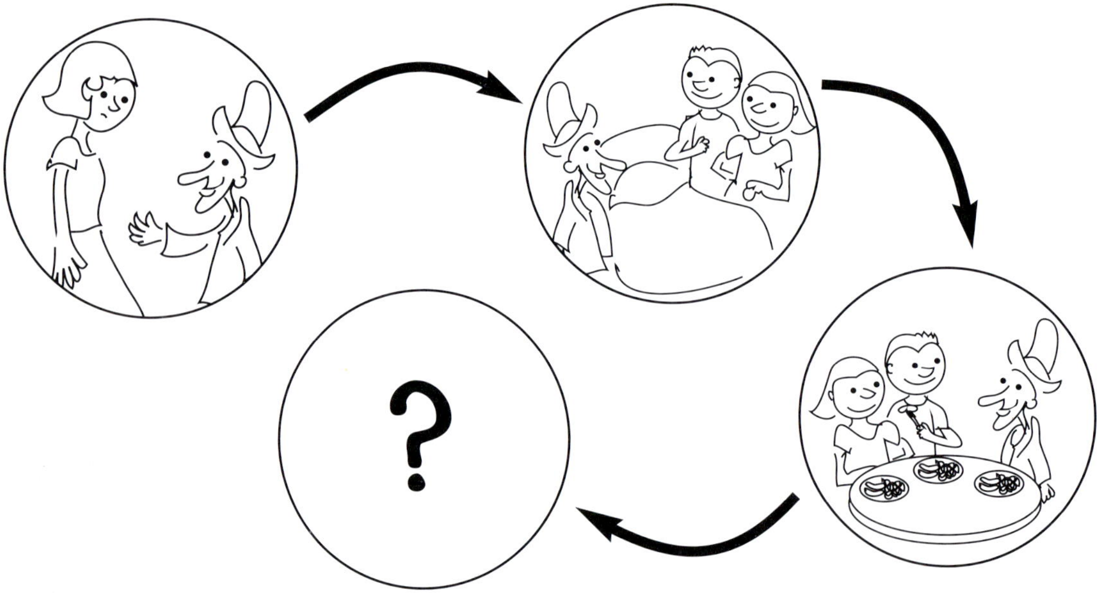

Who do you think the little man is?
Where do you think he came from?

Imagine that you are interviewing
the little man. What five questions
would you ask him? Write these on
a separate piece of paper.

Now imagine that you
are the little man and
answer the questions.

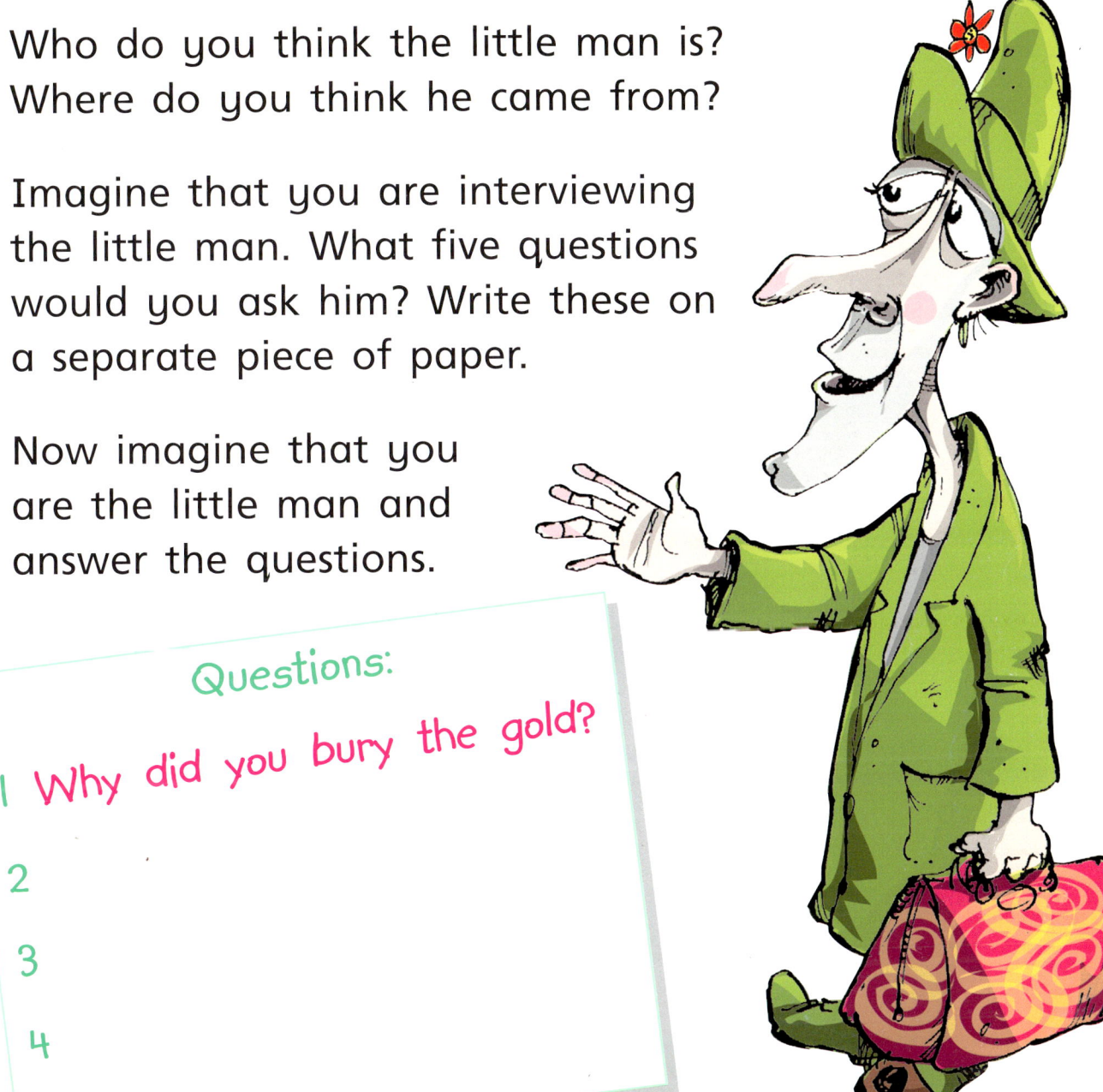

Questions:

1 Why did you bury the gold?

2

3

4

5

Activities

Look at the pictures and think of words to describe the characters.

Have you ever had an argument like Sandy and Bonny?

What advice would you give them to stop them arguing?

Think of a time when you had an argument with a friend.
Can you remember why you argued?

How would you deal with the argument now if the same one happened again?

Charity sale

A charity is a group that collects money for a particular cause, such as people in need. Can you think of a charity that you would like to help? Check with an adult that he or she is happy for you to hold a charity sale.

1 Look around your house. Find any toys, books or clothes that you no longer use. Put them into a box.

2 Write a list of all the things in the box. Write a price next to each item.

3 Write the prices on labels and attach them to each item.

30

4 Invite your friends to your charity sale. Tell them when and where the sale will take place.

5 Have fun at the sale!

6 Count up the money that you have made for your chosen charity.

7 You have raised money for a good cause and made your friends happy – well done!

Parents' and carers' notes

Becoming a confident reader can open up a whole new world to your child. Reading should always be fun.

- Look at the cover together and talk about the title and the picture.

- Look at the pictures and see if your child can predict what the story will be about.

- Encourage your child to read the story to you. Help him or her sound out any difficult words.

- Look at pages 24–25 and help your child retell the story in his or her own words.

- Help your child to complete the activities on pages 26–29. These activities revisit the story and give your child an opportunity to talk about what happened.

- Help your child to host his or her own charity sale as on pages 30–31. This is a great way to talk about the importance of sharing and giving.

- 'The Pot of Gold' is about making choices and realising that our choices have consequences. It also reminds us to be tolerant of friends, family and strangers.

Check that your child can find and read the following interest words in the story. Encourage him or her to vary expression when reading aloud, using the punctuation as a guide.

Interest words: arguing, evening, ragged, gleaming, suppose, temper, hunted